About the Author

I'm a retired United Reformed Church Minister, now living in Dorset. My background is as a speech and drama teacher specialising in work with people who have learning difficulties and as a counsellor and psychotherapist. I have three children and eight grandchildren and I'm still very active.

Emily and Other Stories

Ann G. McNair

Emily and Other Stories

Olympia Publishers
London

www.olympiapublishers.com
OLYMPIA PAPERBACK EDITION

A CIP catalogue record for this title is
available from the British Library.

ISBN: 978-1-78830-592-1

This is a work of creative nonfiction. The events are portrayed to the
best of the author's memory. While all the stories in this book are
true, some names and identifying details have been changed to
protect the privacy of the people involved.

First Published in 2020

Olympia Publishers
Tallis House
2 Tallis Street
London
EC4Y 0AB
Printed in Great Britain

Life Goes On

It was getting near to our daughter's wedding day. Everything was in place and I was trying to finish some gardening duties before the big day, when the phone rang. I dropped what I was doing and rushed inside, as usual running too fast and tripping in the kitchen to land flat against the cooker, ker-plunk! Within a few seconds I realised something had given way by the distinct smell of gas. I quickly answered the phone, telling the person I would have to ring off as I needed to ring the gas board. The few seconds it took to reach them seemed like an eternity but they were very calming and told me exactly what to do to turn the gas off, and reassured me they would be here soon. I didn't have time at that moment to feel how stupid I must have seemed not to know.

The outcome was that new copper piping was required to fit along the breakfast room and into the kitchen to reach behind the cooker. Not before time, as the old lead pipes could not stand the strain.

The wedding came and was soon over. A joyful occasion for us all. The happy couple had a day or two to take their presents over to their new home and to come with my husband and I to choose their wedding album photographs. The honeymoon had initially been cancelled because the bridegroom's mother was very ill and actually died a few weeks before the wedding. We had gone to Yorkshire for the funeral, which my husband as minister presided over and the families coming together at this time helped to lift the spirits considerably, before we returned to London to focus afresh on the plans for the wedding. At the last minute our son-in-law managed to arrange some time away for himself and his bride, so that was another light on the horizon.

Now that our visitors had gone home – some relatives to Scotland, a number to Yorkshire and even two who had come from Devon – we began to unwind and reflect on what had been a hectic but rather wonderful time, with a few things still to sort out. Most of the wedding cake was still to be cut up, with letters of thanks to be sent out and 'good wish' calls to be returned.

It was now the beginning of August, with apples and soft fruit almost ready for picking, so I ventured out into the garden where I knew there was one gardening job that still had to be done. That completed I swithered whether to take the bags of weeds to the tip then or wait till after lunch as I felt in need of a break. In another minute I would have been gone but an anxious call from the house set me running. The freezer motor had caught fire and wooden panelling in the breakfast room was already in flames. I somehow managed to pull the freezer out into the garden as my husband had managed to unplug it and, while I got the dogs to safety, he rang the fire brigade. By now the fire was taking hold and, following instructions, we now got out of the house and waited for help.

The first to arrive were the 'papers', with the risk assessors in toe. Some neighbours, becoming anxious, must have rung the fire brigade also because in the end three turned up almost at the same time.

The dogs led by Bruce, the larger of the two, led the smaller dog Cloe, right round the street, up the service road and into the garden by the back gate. Well done, Bruce! They didn't fully understand and were obviously concerned about the fire, so to help us all our neighbour agreed to have the dogs in her house for a time. Unfortunately, she brought them out into her garden with rope attached to their collars where, if anything, they had an even better view of ourselves and the burning house. Eventually she took them inside where they could settle down and stop barking. It took time for the fire to be brought under control.

We managed to find a temporary place for our beloved dogs that night but sadly our big Bruce was found dead in the morning. He was getting on a bit but the vet said he thought he had died of shock. He was always very protective of the little dog, Cloe who now became unfriendly towards the young man who had brought their breakfast, obviously thinking he may have done something to Bruce. They had been put together in the same kennel. He was a great loss to the family.

Whatever was not burned by the fire had smoke damage, in many cases irretrievably so. We were, for the moment, left with the clothes we were standing up in giving time for what came next. We were shocked, but unhurt apart from singed hair and eyebrows. Later, we were told that without the new piping, not just our house but the one next door would have exploded with perhaps loss of life as well.

My mother's words telling me to slow down and stop running took on new meaning and I felt less guilty from then on because I had been myself and my fall had been used in an unimaginable way for good. We salvaged everything we could, so there was much scrubbing and sorting out to be done.

Our younger son and his wife had been on holiday, and were due back in a few days. We planned to put a letter through their door letting them know what had happened, so that they would not be anxious. Unfortunately, the weather was so bad, they decided to return earlier and promptly ran into a mutual friend, who offered condolences on what had happened to mum and dad. Our son, thinking we had been killed, went into shock, and was unable to respond immediately to the news. The person seeing the effect, and thinking, they already knew about the fire, quietly left them to pick up the pieces. Not knowing what to expect, and with the telephone out of action, they made their way to our home, only to find it barricaded up with a large padlock in place. As we hadn't as yet been found alternative accommodation, we were still staying with neighbours, and saw them arrive. Needless to say, what followed was traumatic, but ended better than was supposed.

The happy couple arrived back in due course to be met by myself and our younger son, who, as sensitively as we were able, told them what had happened. We had to admit that their lovely wedding cake had gone, but they would not hear of a replacement. In any tragedy there always seem to be instances where one can see the lighter side of things, and this was our experience now. Our good neighbour, making us a meal that night, asked if 'chargrilled burgers' were alright for dinner? She quickly realised what she had said, and we began to smile. This was recalled several times afterwards and we would laugh.

A man from the telephone exchange came asking to see the telephone, as it had been reported there was strange noises coming from the line. Eventually we persuaded him that there was no longer a telephone, but we would gladly show him where it had been. He duly reported his findings to the exchange, after sealing off, the damaged wiring.

Someone came to see the video recorder, which at the time, we were renting, and repeatedly banged on the door, and asked about the people living there. We came out of our neighbour's house to explain, then undid the padlock, and led him to the video recorder, which fortunately had remained more or less intact. He didn't seem to understand that the house was uninhabitable. So many more instances, such as this, occurred in the five months it took to renovate our house. The last being, when someone quite seriously asked, if we would be having a 'housewarming party' when we moved back in.

The saddest outcome of all this was the loss of our beloved Bruce. To lose possessions is one thing but loss of life is another. Bruce was so protective of the little one and it was obvious she missed him too. Our temporary home was just a few miles away, opposite the park, so it was easier to take little Cloe for walks. If she saw a dog that resembled Bruce on the other side of the park, she would race towards it only to discover it wasn't him and come racing back. A heart-wrenching moment for us all.

It was Christmas Eve and we had just moved back into our house. The smell of paint was strong, so all the windows were left open, but that could not conceal the overwhelming smell of gas coming from the bathroom. The gas man came only to tell us that the main pipe running behind what had been nicely panelled down one corner was not connected and the reading was off the scale. This put right and the windows closed, we began to feel a little warmer.

Now I decided to be up-beat about facing any difficulties that presented themselves. I had a final paper to finish. It should have been submitted earlier; I had been given an extension because of the fire with the usual jokes about what some people will do for an excuse. It was now a priority if I had any hope of passing my diploma in systemic therapy. After four years study I was not giving up easily.

My monologue 'The Launderette' followed soon after and it is all true exactly as I have written, apart from changing my husband's name, and I admit I do know the difference between rotisserie and rotary clothes dryer. For me it turned, what could have been a miserable day, into an amusing experience. It was once in print, but without what led up to it being known.

The Launderette

I did have one of those rotis… rot… rotisserie clothes dryers. You know the sort that goes up like an umbrella turned inside out; but they kept disappearing. You know what I mean, they sank into the lawn… Well it's not a lawn really, just a bit of knobbly grass and so in the end Alfred said, "Let's do it properly – what I propose," he's good at proposing things, Alfred is, "is to dig a hole in the grass, a foot square and a foot deep, and then pour a load of concrete in, and while it's still soft, imbed the base of the dryer into it."

Well to make sure nothing went wrong, we indulged ourselves and bought a new one. Well Alfred dug his hole, did the concrete bit and got the base of the dryer really planted in it, and it did work a treat until the business with the house. You remember, we had to have the builders in to put things right. I don't know what they did with it, but the first time I put my washing on it after they'd gone, it collapsed on top of me – snapped sheer off! I think they must have been swinging on it.

So there I was with a load of wet clothes, and that's why I had to go to the launderette.

They don't really like you going in to dry things when you haven't used the machines, so I peeped in, nonchalantly, no attendant, so I went in.

There were only two women chatting in a corner, said hello and nodded, and immediately they started to talk louder, and you know you can't help hearing.

One said, "I had to lie down when they took it"

"Did you? Oh I didn't. I just sat in a chair."

"Well I think it was because they had diagnosed other things that were wrong with me."

"Oh – did they give you any pills to take?"

"Yes."

"And are you still taking them?"

"Oh yes."

"When I went back they said I wouldn't have to take them anymore, my blood pressure was normal."

"No, they told me right from the start. Mrs Gall, they said, you'll have to take these pills for the rest of your life."

Then I had to put more money in the machine.

"They made me lie down with a sheet thing over me and they brought this great metal thing down on top of me, and you know that huge man in the 007 film with the metal teeth, it made me think of him and I couldn't help giggling."

Then it was time to feed the machine again.

"They gave me the operation without an anaesthetic."

"What! They did the operation without any anaesthetic? Wasn't it painful?"

"Well it was a bit. They just froze the spot and gave me a kind of locum injection, and I was fully conscious throughout."

"Oh I've never heard of them doing that operation without an anaesthetic. What happened?"

"Well, they made a hole in my head and then they pulled. You know what it's like when someone grabs you by the scruff of the neck and pulls you up, it felt just like that; and I could feel myself going – woo! Oh it was a funny sensation."

Well just at that moment a man came in, not to use the dryers but to shelter from the rain and watch the folk coming from the school. If the attendant had been there she'd probably have told him to get on his way, but he wasn't doing any harm. I mean he wasn't vandalising the machines or being rude. He just stood there. Seeing the school was out, I looked at my watch and realised I was procrastinating, so I gathered up the clothes, said goodbye to the two women who were still standing there and made off home. Oh yes, it's a funny world, isn't it?

A Thought

Nowadays, we take our holidays at different times throughout the year. The fact that summer is, according to the calendar, over here, means it is the beginning of summer somewhere else. If skiing is your pleasure? Happy days! Just try not to break anything. If you are still waiting to have your break (excuse the pun) or trying to catch up before winter sets in, then I hope it will be as stress free and rewarding as possible.

We try to make life good as it should be, and are often greatly saddened by the things we read about or see on our televisions. We reflect on our lives, we make plans but if problems arise hopefully, we know what our priorities are.

We know we cannot turn a blind eye to all the terrible things that are happening daily in our own country as well as countries throughout the world. As human beings our instinct might be to wipe out the oppressors with significant force to right the wrong, but as we all know things are never as straight forward as they sometimes appear in the newspaper reports and anyway who are we to judge or think we have all the answers to man's ills?

Before we do things we would regret, as Christians we have to turn it all over to the only one who has the answers to the intricacies of human behaviour. We need to draw on our belief in God who wants his people to be at peace, to be free and living in harmony with one another – sharing the good things in life and gaining strength from the knowledge of his abundant love, mercy and forgiveness.

We all have our part to play, no matter how remote from it all we imagine ourselves to be. When we see clearly how truly blessed we are, we will have taken a necessary step to being involved in overcoming the mindless violence and utter cruelty which is no match for the goodness and power of God.

Boy

A solitary dog barked, that deep bark that belonged there, and without looking we knew it was Boy telling us that the butcher's van had arrived, or that another dog had wandered in and that he would deal with it.

At the second bark, the drama would be too much and we would look, with the mind dancing frantically to know the reason.

Mostly it would all be over by that time, with the offending dog well on its way, and Boy finishing his round of the grass patch in front of the church or, if all was quiet, stretching out for a nap in some convenient spot before lunch.

Walnut

Walnut! That's it! That's what the boy's name, which for the life of me I can't remember at present, reminds me of.

I can still see him walking down the hill and round the corner, violin case tucked neatly under one arm, always navy raincoat, wellington boots and glasses, his smooth dark hair neatly brushed round his pale white face.

He wasn't ill, or indeed a sickly youth to my knowledge, just quiet and somehow alone.

His classmates laughed at him or pitied him, which wasn't a very satisfactory position to be in, but it seemed as though part of him remained unaffected by the lack of friendship about him.

I felt a deep sadness somewhere in his being which he vainly tried to compensate for by his constant practise, although one had the feeling that inside, he would never really play the music for himself, only for someone else. That along with his somewhat impaired intelligence, which might include a near perfect technique, would have at times a 'dampers down' effect in reverse: like being too loud or too soft but never just right.

Since that was many years ago and I have not seen or heard of him since, I hope I was wrong.

What Do You Think?

People have said to me that Christianity has made no difference to the social life of the people and in fact at times appears to have made things worse. There are still the same problems to be faced today as there were hundreds of years ago.

In October, 1805, Nelson won the battle of Trafalgar and it is thought to be a glorious victory. What we don't hear about is the countless number of people, including children, who were dying like flies in our cotton mills at the time through malnutrition, overwork and flogging – so much so that it became impossible to find places to bury them. Christianity changed all this – not immediately, but in time through people seeing at first hand the inhuman treatment suffered.

Some years ago, I was working in a hospital for mentally and physically disadvantaged women. It was vastly overcrowded with as many as ten women sleeping in one room, without proper facilities, and no privacy. Wreaths brought from funerals by well-meaning patrons were a constant reminder, to most there, of death and their own fragility.

All this changed, not immediately, but through people being made to see first-hand the intolerable conditions these poor souls were suffering. A village for those least able was set up in the grounds of a local hospital. Many of the others were given a place with families where they had their own room for the first time in their lives, with freedom to come and go and their own money to spend.

When we feel compassion, we are in touch with the God in us, which for the Christian means striving always to make a difference.

And So It Was That

On a bitter March day in 1944, Mother remembered the month ever after, as each year she took pains to remind the children what a treacherous month it was and checked to see that they were well.

Her youngest child was ill. The cough she had had for two weeks seemed to have responded to the medicine but now she lay limp and fevered, with her head in the cool corner of a chair, just wishing to fall asleep. She was lifted to bed and made as comfortable as possible.

It was gone midnight when the doctor arrived and his diagnosis was what her mother had feared; what was known as the silent killer, lobar pneumonia. Mother wouldn't hear of her child going into hospital; she would nurse her at home.

To have any chance of recovery someone would have to take the prescription into the centre of the town where there was the only chemist open all night. The men of the family were all away fighting in the war. She couldn't leave the children and there could be an air raid.

The extended family lived too far away and nobody had a telephone. She had never prayed harder than she did that night. A gentle knock at the door focused her attention. She opened it to find cousin Grace, who sometimes paid a visit though not usually at such a late hour. Grace willingly made the journey and duly arrived back with the M&Bs to begin the battle for the little girl's life. The only other medicine available at the time was the antibiotic, penicillin, which was mostly kept for wounded service people, but in this case the child was allergic to it. As a result, the recovery was much greater, with no guarantee the patient would survive the crisis.

It took many weeks, but at last the fever broke and slowly the child began to get well.

So many good friends with support and loving prayers and of course dear Grace arriving just in time that night and Mother there day and night giving complete care and all for one little life. Who could say they don't believe in miracles?

Lower Largo

At some time in our lives we will experience a desire to retrace our steps, either literally or in memory, to an earlier time and place.

A few years ago I went back to the Fife Coast to a little fishing village called Lower Largo, where I had spent many childhood holidays. It is very near Lundin Links and quite near to St. Andrews, both well known to golfing enthusiasts.

No fish are caught and sold there now. Its streets and houses have had a face lift but the old haunts are still recognisable. The railway station and tracks have given way to a cliff path with grass and wild flowers. The only hotel is at the end of the pier and this has been extended and is very comfortable, with fine cuisine. There are only a few shops, displaying local crafts, and a tea room with home-made cakes and regional delicacies.

However, Largo has its own claim to fame. In the middle of the main street (there is only one) stands the house of Alexander Selkirk, better known to most as Robinson Crusoe, with a statue of the famous figure outside.

For me this journey back was a wonderful experience. There are the happy memories of course and an almost magical feeling, recalling treasured times with grandparents and friends.

It is said that we cannot go back to recapture an earlier time in life and this is true because life changes as people do and hopefully we ourselves mature with the years.

Sometimes there is a need to ‘lay ghosts’ from the past, or relive an experience in order to move on. There are many strands that knit together to make a life and remembering can be an affirming and refreshing experience.

We cannot actually relive the past but we can bring back the good feelings, experience them and use them for our life in the present.

Whatever our reason for such a journey, be assured that God will be with us and, as our spirits are refreshed, we can feel once again that part of ourselves, linking lives through the years and on into eternity.

Careful Wording

I have bandaged your foot but it may fall off at any moment. Is it the bandage or the foot that may fall off? Only those involved would have any idea whether it meant losing either or both.

I am reminded of Benjamin Franklin's words: 'For the want of a nail the shoe was lost, for the want of a shoe the horse was lost, for the want of a horse the rider was lost, for the want of a rider the battle was lost'.

Do we look deeply enough at what has happened and make sure that any wound is recognised and given full attention?

When I was three I fell on a brick path, was taken to hospital where stitches were applied to my nose, ointment to other cuts and a penny in my little hand for being brave and not crying.

Only in recent years did I discover the central partition in my nose was bent which caused pain when I used my upper range in singing, and no doubt is responsible for nose blockage and more on occasion, – no need to go into it.

When we try to help someone, we listen to the thing that causes them pain. It may be anxiety, even guilt or it may be a deeper wound that even they are unaware of.

If the person can become his or her own therapist, accepting of themselves as they would of another, gently probing the deeper levels of consciousness, almost like a puzzle with many of the pieces hopefully beginning to come to light. Never condemning but watching out for the red light and taking it as an indicator of discovery that some significant point has been reached. Then stop, rest and wait until the curiosity to seek more answers returns. No one likes to leave a puzzle unfinished.

It can be helpful to take this journey of discovery alongside someone who has only your well-being at heart. Choose well and never forget that God knows what really needs to happen for the sore parts to be truly helped and healed.

Jacob

Jacob was the elder son of a lovely Jewish couple who were anxious about their son's progress at school. He had ability and a friendly disposition but he found it difficult to fit in with his peers. Word gets around and I was approached and asked if I could help.

Two things quickly emerged. First, Jacob lacked the quiet confidence needed to face more self-composed young people who appeared to take life in their stride and secondly, when he was annoyed with himself for not trying to answer his teacher's questions when an opportunity arose. Then at other times rushing with answers not fully formed in his mind, only to finish up feeling stupid.

Speech work to develop his voice and help dispel anxiety, then finding out what his interests were, getting him to talk about them and in this way for him to feel affirmed. Gradually we got on to things which he didn't approve of and letting him say why. Sometimes he could write about something which had happened which had left him feeling down or wronged. He began to open up and felt trusted to talk about many things. If I didn't altogether agree about something, we could discuss it and often a compromise was reached where things weren't black or white but, depending on circumstances, would seem somewhere in between.

He had been to Spain and seen a bull fight which he considered horrific and barbaric. He had taken mental notes of the whole thing from beginning to end and spoke with much feeling and true emotion on the subject.

We agreed this would make a fine talk which he could give in a Spoken English exam for LAMDA. We worked on refining the details and, with new found confidence, this was the next step. It all went well, and proved to be the beginning of a new phase in his life.

His parents had their own business and now they were happy with the thought that their son could become involved in it and hopefully, one day take it over.

A happy outcome for all concerned.

Beth

Beth was an only child and was very precious to her mother and father. She was a beautiful baby with no indication that she would be anything less than a perfect child. As time went by however, it became obvious that something was wrong. Nothing was diagnosed. It could have been slight damage at birth although nothing had been amiss and in the end it was accepted that they would probably never have the answers they looked for.

My name had been given as someone who worked with people with special needs but also taught speech and drama for The London Academy and would be happy to work with the child. I found at times that Beth seemed not to hear what I was saying to her. Her hearing was tested, but the consultants could find nothing wrong. Her parents had already noticed this lack of response. Beth appeared to respond to familiar objects and words and was learning by rote. Repeating sounds she liked.

Beth had a good speech mechanism and enjoyed stories and poetry, so there was a lot of interest to work with. Beth enjoyed making noises by banging with sticks or spoons on anything she found. Her parents had brought her a small drum to play on, but she would quickly lose interest. I suggested to her parents that by partially filling tins of different sizes, with pulses, seeds or nuts, any sound they might make for Beth's pleasure, could be stimulating and fun. The same thing could be done with different containers, and used as rattles.

Beth's movement was restless, but with music and singing, we were able to give her the chance to move freely in any pattern she liked, at any given moment.

The finger patterns, which had made her parents anxious (mainly drumming with her fingers separately for some time, in quick frantic movements, on different surfaces) they now accepted as Beth's way of pushing forward in her development. I suggested paper fans might be an option to introduce, if possible.

She was quick to learn words and developed a strong clear voice. Eventually she could sit comfortably on the floor and entertain us by reciting a poem. Beth could say the lines of a poem with exactly the correct feeling and expression, as she had heard me say them to her. Although I wondered at first how much she had understood fully. Every week I felt she understood and appreciated more meaning, but not always sustained through the next lesson. I felt that if it was possible for Beth to pass a poetry test, it would increase confidence in her ability for family and school alike. Her parents were delighted at the thought, if a little apprehensive, but felt they could trust me to make the decision. I knew the Academy would give her every chance to do her best and disperse little fears.

I wrote a covering letter explaining that she might sit on the floor to recite but hopefully by that time she would be able to stand up reasonably straight.

She did sit on the floor for one of the pieces but the wonderful thing was that she passed and was awarded a certificate, much to the delight of all.

Beth continued to progress at school and later was chosen to compete in the Paralympics. A wonderful achievement! I wish her and her parents all good wishes for future further fulfilment in their family life.

Where Now

Sam was dyslexic at a time when little was known about the difficulty. If a person was fortunate enough to be 'given their head' in circumstances where money was not an issue, clever enough to work out what needed to be done to overcome the hindrance and attain a high standard of education. For most, it meant feeling a bit of a dunce, sitting in a corner with very little serious help from anyone around and later finding work where it was not an issue so they could earn a living.

Sam was by no means stupid. He had learned to drive and held down a job which gave him a sense of being. With a deep-seated problem waiting to be resolved and feeling the need of much comfort eating, he now weighed twenty-four stone and, to add to that, he was blind in one eye.

Starting at the beginning seemed logical. He could write his name but had difficulty telling one letter from another and so we began, making a game of it as we went along, giving back the confidence and hopefully some fun as we progressed. I introduced children's books he would have longed to read, but found beyond him.

Gradually, the confusion that lay at the heart of everything came to light. He knew who his mother was but because he couldn't call her mother in public, (he was known to most people as her nephew) one can only imagine the tearing that took place in his being. Gradually, through gentle consultation, a new understanding and agreement was reached and the longed-for healing could begin.

Over years of nonverbal communication with his dearest wish, now a reality, he at last began to think seriously about his weight and consulted a doctor. He was told that, if he didn't take on board what was advised now, he had only six months to live.

He went into hospital and after a year under a strict regime he had lost twelve stone in weight. While there he met the lady who was to become his wife. It sounds like a fairy-tale ending. Now he had the hope of marriage and having a family of his own. Something he could only have imagined before.

His mother came up trumps and Sam was secure for life. He was now living with his mother in her home. I imagine there had been little time for progress in his learning, while he was in hospital, but his case was now brought to those who could possibly secure him future help, and with his permission, he was entered into courses, with the prospect of a more fulfilling life opening up for him, in the future.

I was invited to the wedding, which took place in a beautiful old church in a country setting. All went well, and I admit I was so happy with the outcome. It had taken seven years to bring us to this point in the young man's life.

To Listen

Lewis was the eldest of three siblings. He had been a big baby and extra long compared to the average, so it was reckoned he would be at least six foot four inches tall. Normally this would not be a cause for concern for both parents were a good height but the fact that Lewis had phenylketonuria, which in most cases was detected at birth, had remained unknown for some months by which time there was considerable damage to the brain.

He was a beautiful child and by the time I saw him at the age of seven or eight he was almost uncontrollable. He would sit on the floor and kick out at anyone who came near, then empty boxes of toys and throw the contents at random.

In the room where we met there was a piano which he would bang relentlessly with his hands. When someone played a tune, he would listen then push them aside and begin to bang on the piano himself.

I always felt something of his unhappiness, almost as though he was telling the world, "This is not how things should be. It was with this thought I went to work.

His mother was lovely but I realised she was afraid to chastise her son, but was in fact giving him approval when he was naughty to try and make him feel accepted and loved. She was always in the room with him, apologetically picking up the pieces her son threw.

As gently as I was able, I told her that it appeared Lewis was trying to please her by being so disruptive, and that a gentle reprimand might begin to change things for the better. It was a first step and I felt that if Lewis could begin to see the effect his behaviour had on others, it might make him more aware of his family's love and their consideration for him.

It worked and when I felt the time was right I sat with him in an empty room to see if there would be any indication that all the talking I had done with speech exercises, music and saying the names of things as I pointed to them (for he had never spoken at all) had made any impression.

I sat there thinking, 'If you won't talk to me I won't talk to you.'

He began by shifting his position around the room, trying to get me to respond. Finally he stared at me then calmly began spitting on the seat of one of the chairs until he had made a large pool in the centre then, as there was no response from me he began to tilt the chair so that the pool of spittle began to fall to the floor. I got up, took him by the hand without saying a word and together we walked to the kitchen, found a suitable cloth and went back to the room where I took his hand in mine and together we mopped the floor. Before we finished, I gave him a gentle smack on the back of his hand and said firmly, "No."

This seemed to be the breakthrough. The next time I saw them his mother reported that Lewis had begun to play with his younger brother and sister and things were much happier overall. Shortly after this Lewis said "Good morning" to a shopkeeper. It was first time he had spoken to anyone. His mother could hardly contain herself as he repeated the greeting. The shopkeeper, not thinking anything of it, had ignored the first words but when it had sunk in there were tears of joy all round.

A small step for some but a massive one for Lewis.

Emily

It all began when a group of women from our church started to visit patients in a nearby hospital for those considered unable either mentally, physically or too troublesome to cope with the outside world and were probably there for life. Their ages ranged from youngsters in their teens to very old age

With very limited space, Matron did a marvellous job and had organised the women, broadly speaking into two groups. There were the Girls and the Children. Each of us was happy to take on one of the ladies usually one of the 'Girls' as the 'Children' had more complex needs and were not always aware of those around them.

This is when I met Emily, who was by then in her early fifties. She was needy, institutionalised and accepting of her life in the hospital, and here we were at the end of the 1960s and nothing had changed.

Emily had grown up in what appeared to be a loving family. She was an only child and developed St Vitas Dance quite early on. Her mother had TB and Emily had to sleep with her until her mother died. Her father seemed quite close to Emily, who made quite a good recovery but still had learning difficulties which he found hard to cope with alone. He was a well-known estate agent in the area and found no difficulty in choosing another wife. However, things didn't work out and at the age of nineteen, Emily was committed to the hospital, where she had lived ever since. Her new mother was Scottish and, since I am Scottish, let's say it took some time to establish trust between us.

I visited her once a week and a bond was formed. The patients were each given a little money to spend every month and the more able ones had someone to take them shopping for small things they fancied. Most of the ladies couldn't sign their names so there were many Xs in the books. Naturally the ladies were asked to sign their names when they received the bit of money each month. The Xs were allowed for those who couldn't write their names. I was given permission to teach them and a blackboard, chalk and writing materials were found. Every week there was great excitement as many of them learned to write their names for the first time.

As time went on, I was allowed to take Emily into town for tea and a little shopping and, later, a special meal on her birthday.

At first she would shout out things on the bus about people who had hurt her in some remembered incident from childhood, but gradually she learned to be more serene and keep anything she had the need to say until we were alone.

I discovered she was artistic so we would take a trip to a nice spot where she could draw in the quietness for some time until she became anxious or confused and then it was time to go back home. One day, I was delighted to be presented with two beautiful drawings she had copied from the lid of a chocolate box.

There were times when she thought I could take her home to live with me but, after careful explanation, she understood and was content. The times when my attention was with the larger group, for I had developed a session where most of the ladies could join in, when the writing was finished, with stories, poems, singing with some music and movement, Emily seemed eager to share with the odd remark aside, “She is my lady.”

Even after years of requests for things to change, the patients were still living in very cramped conditions, in some cases ten to a room with a lot of unhappiness when one took another’s hairbrush or a quarrel broke out. The matron must have been a saint to be able to hold it all together.

Eventually the authorities were convinced and a village was set up in the grounds of a local hospital and the less able women were moved there with some rejoicing for all concerned.

Emily was given a room of her own in a family house in Ealing. She was now a pensioner, with a little money of her own, and had the choice of mingling with the family or staying quietly by herself. I wanted to leave all that we had shared with her and only twice was I contacted to go and see her. We had tea and talked of all she had now and the difference it had made to her life. She could come and go as she pleased, with loving friends about her. She particularly appreciated seeing the children in the house growing up. It was almost like a second chance to be truly herself.